To my dad, Simpson Bobo Tanner

— S.T.C.

Library of Congress Cataloging-in-Publication Data
Chitwood, Suzanne.
Wake up, big barn / by Suzanne Chitwood.
p.   cm.
"Cartwheel Books."
Summary: Rhyming text describes a rowdy, rollicking farm where piggies love a mud bath,
farm frogs rock hop, and Owl's on the night shift, shooby, hooby, hoo!
ISBN 0-439-26627-0 (POB)
[1. Farm life—Fiction. 2. Domestic animals—Fiction. 3. Stories in rhyme.] I. Title.
PZ7.K55964Sh 1998
[E]—dc21   2001032778

10 9 8 7 6 5 4 3 2 1   02 03 04 05 06
Printed in Singapore 46
First printing, April 2002

The illustrations in this book were created using
torn papers from catalogs and magazines.
The text type was set in Candida.
Book design by Patti Ann Harris.

suzanne tanner chitwood

Wake Up, Big Barn!

Cartwheel
·B·O·O·K·S·®

SCHOLASTIC INC.
New York   Toronto   London   Auckland   Sydney
Mexico City   New Delhi   Hong Kong   Buenos Aires

Wake up, Big Barn!

Cock-
a-
doodle-
doo!

Piggies love

a mud bath.

Hee-haw,   hee-haw!

Moo, moo,

moo!

Wiggle,
wiggle
weather vane,
windy day.

Show

me

your

feathers.

Neigh,
neigh,
HAY!

Hip-hop, be^{bop},

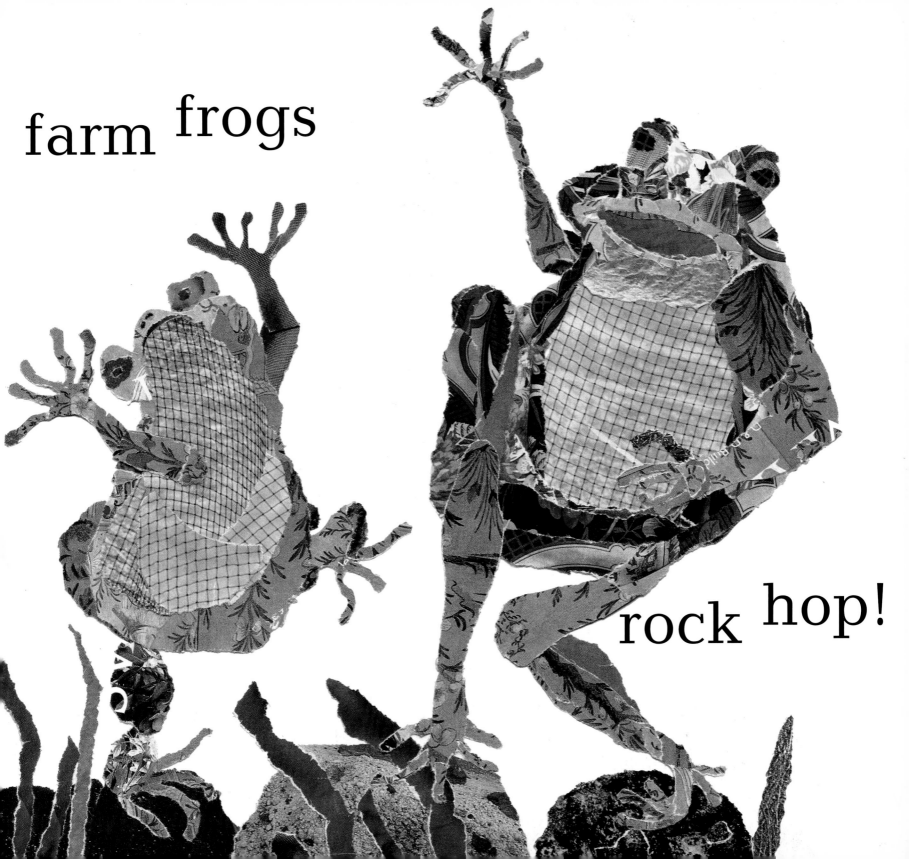

farm frogs

rock hop!

Corn time,

snack time,

pop

pop

pop

pop!

Wheels
stop
chugga-ching.

Flap,

flap,

fly!

Cherries fall,

ping,

ping!

Let's eat pie!

Owl's on the night shift,
shooby,
hooby,
hoo!

Good night,
Big Barn!
Good night,
you!